For you. For all of it. For Olivette.

For all of you. For all love. For all love, it is you. —N.T.

For my Maddie—this book was as much a labor of love as you were. —M.K.

All rights reserved. Published in the United States by Random House Children's Books, a division of Penguin Random House LLC, New York.

Random House and the colophon are registered trademarks of Penguin Random House LLC.

Visit us on the Web! rhcbooks.com

Educators and librarians, for a variety of teaching tools, visit us at RHTeachersLibrarians.com

Library of Congress Cataloging-in-Publication Data is available upon request.
ISBN 978-0-593-38153-3 (hardcover) — ISBN 978-0-593-38154-0 (lib. bdg.) — ISBN 978-0-593-38155-7 (ebook)

The artist used Adobe Photoshop to create the illustrations for this book.
The text of this book is set in 16-point Rockwell Regular.
Interior design by Nicole Gastonguay

MANUFACTURED IN CHINA
10 9 8 7 6 5 4 3 2
First Edition

Olivette is YOU

Nico Tortorella

Illustrations by
Melissa Kashiwagi

Random House 🏠 New York

AUTHOR'S NOTE

I've always known that I was going to be a parent. When my partner, Bethany, and I first met as teenagers, we could clearly imagine a future with children. What we never imagined were all the struggles and triumphs that come with creating life in a fragile world in the most fragile of times.

The idea for the character of Olivette came to me in a dream at the beginning of our fertility journey. The spirit of a child who represented all the parts of myself. My past, my present, my future. Constantly evolving. With the ability to bend so it is impossible for us to break.

Olivette is all of it—the entirety of the universe that exists in each and every one of us. Not here or there, nor this or that, but in between and beyond. Olivette is the messy and magnificent and the neat and tidy parts that make each one of us unique and who we are.

To all the parents and grandparents and family members and chosen family and friends and everyone in the whole world . . . Olivette is you. As you read this book to the little one in your life, I encourage you to imagine the Olivette that exists in each and every one of us. You are the question, the answer, the possibility, the impossible, the absurdity, and the reason. Everything in the entire world needed to happen in order for you to be right here right now, with this book, with this love, no matter what. And it is still happening. . . .

All of it is you. All love, it is you.
In gratitude, always,

Nico

My name is Olivette,
And all of it is me.
I have special powers
To be all I want to be.
I am Olivette,
And all of it is me!

Some days I feel so happy:
Smiling, in a great mood.

Some days I feel so grumpy:
Frowning and very blue.
All *my* feelings are *me*.
And everything *you* feel is *you*.

Some days I feel like a queen,
Some days I feel like a king.

I am the space between it all,
So today I'll dress just like me!
That is my favorite way to show
I am each, any, and *every*thing.

Water reminds me of me,
How it moves from state to state:

Sometimes I skate,
Or cook,
Or swim.
Somehow they all relate!

And just as water is fluid,
Going from ice to gas to wet,

I can be anything and all of it:
I am ever-changing Olivette!

But I am not the only one
To contain such different parts.
You and I are quite similar,
Just look inside our hearts.

We are all connected,
Part of this great big universe.
Each one made by a higher power:
No one better, no one worse.

All of us are special,
Unique and individual.

We come in all shapes and colors,
Yet all of us are equal.

No matter where we come from,
What we look like,
How we speak,

We aren't that different, after all.
We are equally unique!

We're the future's hopes and dreams,
And change begins with us.
A world embracing everyone
Is accepting, wise, and just.

My love flows from me,
And it goes straight to you!
Loving is my special power,
And you can share it, too.

All of it is you.
And all love,
It is you.